POEMS JUST FOR ME

POEMS BY THE SEA

Chosen by Brian Moses

Illustrated by Marcela Calderón

WINDMILL BOOKS

Published in 2018 by Windmill Books, an Imprint of Rosen Publishing
29 East 21st Street, New York, NY 10010

Editor: Victoria Brooker
Designer: Lisa Peacock

Acknowledgments: The Compiler and Publisher would like to thank the authors for allowing their poems to appear in
this anthology. Poems © the authors. While every attempt has been made to gain permissions and provide an up-to-date
biography, in some cases this has not been possible and we apologize for any omissions. Should there be any inadvertent
omission, please apply to the Publisher for rectification.

Cataloging-in-Publication Data
Names: Moses, Brian.
Title: Poems by the sea / compiled by Brian Moses.
Description: New York : Windmill Books, 2018. | Series: Poems just for me | Includes index.
Identifiers: ISBN 9781499483925 (pbk.) | ISBN 9781499483888 (library bound) | ISBN 9781508193159 (6 pack)
Subjects: LCSH: Sea poetry. | Marine animals--Juvenile poetry. | Children's poetry, American.
Classification: LCC PR6058.U37 P64 2018 | DDC 821'.914--dc23

Manufactured in China
CPSIA Compliance Information: Batch #BS17WM: For Further Information contact Rosen Publishing, New York, New York at 1-800-237-9932

Contents

Are We Nearly There Yet?

When we went to the seaside this year
my little sister just wouldn't be quiet.

Again and again
she kept on asking,
"Are we nearly there yet?"

We drove to the end of our street
and my sister said,
"Are we nearly there yet?"

We left the town behind
and again she said,
"Are we nearly there yet?"

We stopped for a train to go by
and my sister called,
"Are we nearly there yet?"

We sped along the motorway
and my sister said,
"Are we nearly there yet?"
We stopped for something to eat
and my sister grumbled,
"Are we nearly there yet?"

We waited in a line of cars
and my sister screamed,
"ARE WE NEARLY THERE YET?"

We caught a glimpse of the sea
and my sister yawned,
"Are we nearly there yet?"

But when we finally reached the end
of our long and tiring trip,
my sister didn't say anything,
she was fast asleep... zzzzzzz!

Brian Moses

5

Beach Counting

One for the sun that shone in the sky.

Two for the ships that sailed on by.

Three for the castles I built on the sand.

Four for the seashells I held in my hand.

Five for the points on the starfish I saw.

Six for the crabs that scuttled ashore.

Seven for the waves that I managed to beat.

Eight for the pebbles I perched on my feet.

Nine for the boats that bobbed on the sea.

Ten for my toes that were wiggling free.

Tony Mitton

I Do Like to Be Beside the Seaside

Oh! I do like to be beside the seaside
I do like to be beside the sea
I do like to stroll upon the Prom, Prom, Prom,
Where the brass bands play
Tiddely om pom pom!
So just let me be beside the seaside
I'll be beside myself with glee
And there's lots of girls beside,
I should like to be beside,
Beside the seaside!
Beside the sea!

John A. Glover-Kind

The Seagull's Song

Oh! I do like to be beside the seaside
I do like to be beside the sea,
I do like to soar above a seaside town,
See the boats in the harbor bobbing up and down.

Oh! I do like to be beside the seaside
There is nowhere that I would rather be,
I can perch on sailing ships,
Grab a meal of fish and chips,
Beside the seaside, beside the sea.

June Crebbin

9

Seagulls with Everything

You get seagulls with everything
at St. Ives...

Seagulls with walking sticks,
seagulls with glasses,
seagulls with lipstick,
and ones with moustaches.

Seagulls with hats
to cover bald heads,
seagulls with blankets
still lying in bed.

Seagulls with tickets
to travel on trains,
seagulls with telescopes
high up on cranes.

Seagulls with lollies
and ice cream cones,
seagulls with diaries
and mobile phones.

Seagulls in shades
strumming guitars,
seagulls with girlfriends
driving fast cars.

Seagulls with dreams
to fly from St. Ives
and be big movie stars
for the rest of their lives.

Brian Moses

Seaside Sounds

Listen can you hear

    The whisper of the waves brushing the shore

The slip-slop of the flip-flops on the sand

    The fluttering of the flag flapping in the breeze

The splish-splosh of water slopping from a child's bucket

    The raucous squawks of the marauding seagulls

The cries and gasps of bathers as the cold water swirls around them

    The screams and howls as they splash each other

The warning shout of a mother

    The sobbing of the child who has dropped her ice-cream

Granddad's snore as he sleeps in his deckchair.

John Foster

12

A Single Wave

A single wave
knows just how to behave!

A swish,
a swash,
and a swoosh of a leap
then a graceful, white curtsey
performed gently at your feet.

Yes a single wave
knows just how to behave!

Ian Souter

The 7th Wave

first wave   slops slow
hop-step   come-go

second wave pushes
shoves and rushes

wave number three
picks on me

wave four
is all roar

wave five is a breaker
a crashing breath-taker

wave six rises high
is a green and salty sky

the seventh wave's a slammer
a roller-rock-rammer
a beach-bashing
shell-smashing
monster-sized
hammer

Jan Dean

There's an Ocean in this Seashell

There's an ocean in this seashell
That I'm holding to my ear.
As I listen very closely
It's an ocean I can hear.
It is swishing, it is swashing,
It is sloshing all about.
It is splashing, it is thrashing,
It is dashing in and out.

There's an ocean in this seashell,
But wherever can it be?
When I look inside this seashell
There is nothing there to see.
Yet I know it was an ocean
For I heard its mighty roar,
As I listened to this seashell
That I found upon the shore.

Graham Denton

16

Shells

White ones
Pink ones
Rough and smooth and shiny ones,
Big ones,
Small ones
Long and thin and tiny ones
Dust off the sand!
Wash them in the sea!
A bucket full of memories
Coming home with me.

Debra Bertulis

17

Skimming Stones on the Sea

When the sea shimmers still and grey
It's a perfect skim stone day.

Choose a stone that's flat and thin,
Frisbee it and watch it skim.

Skip...

skip...

skip...

Skip,

skip,

skip,

PLOP!

Count the ripples of each hop.

It's a perfect skim stone day
when the sea shimmers still and grey.

Jane Clarke

Treasure Chest Mystery

What could be in the treasure chest,
forgotten at the bottom of the sea?

A diamond ring?
A fine silk scarf?
A bottle of rum to make the sailors laugh?
A silver sword?
A golden crown?
A crumpled map, all soggy and brown?

A beautiful bracelet, blue as the sky?
An old peg-leg?
A patch for an eye?

A wishing-well of wonders
there could be,
forgotten at the bottom of the sea!

Kate Williams

Playtime Pirate (Action Rhyme)

This is my treasure map.   *(pretend to hold a map)*
This is my boat.   *(draw a boat in the air with your finger)*
These are the waves   *(make wave motions with your hands)*
where I rock and float.

There is the island   *(point to an island in the distance)*
I'm headed for.
This is the way   *(mime wading through the water)*
that I wade ashore.

This is the spot.   *(draw an X in front of yourself, point to the ground)*
This is my spade.   *(grip your imaginary shovel)*
This is the deep,   *(dig with your imaginary shovel)*
dark hole I made.

This is the box   *(lift an imaginary box from the hole)*
that I dug from the ground.
And these are the golden   *(fling coins into the air with glee)*
coins I found.

Tony Mitton

Letters in Bottles

I'm stranded on an island.
There's no one else. Just me.
But PLEASE don't send
a rescue ship —
I'm as happy as can be.

In the Under-Sea Museum
(Below the deepest wave)
You'll find a THOUSAND bottles
In a sleepy, creepy cave.
And EACH ONE holds a letter
That was written long ago —
What happened to the writers?
I'm afraid we'll never know...

Across the seas
This note has come.
I'm safe. I'm well.
Please tell my Mum.

Dear Reader,
In your salty hand
You hold a map —
It shows a land
Where TREASURE lies
Beneath the sand.
The X will show you
Where to look. Good luck!
Good digging!
From: C. Hook.

I'm tired. I'm bored.
I'm on a boat,
And all we do
ALL DAY is float.
So here's a note
From me to you.
(The date is 1892.)

You've found my letter!
Write back soon —
This morning, or
This afternoon.
I'll wait. I'll watch
The stormy seas.
I'm VERY lonely.
Write back! Please!

Clare Bevan

The Bucket

Do you remember
that afternoon, dashing
across the sand? Bucket
in hand, net in the other,
then hovering over
every pool? And once
done, we'd hurry back,
bucket now full, everyone
trying to catch a glimpse
of three green crabs,
two little fish,
and all of those
fidgety shrimps?

Then finally strolling
back to sea, wading out,
T-shirts wet, tipping
them into the waves?
How could we
ever forget?

James Carter

25

Rock Pool

Barnacle's on bass guitar,
hermit crab on drums,
starfish does the singing
and a shrimp guitarist strums.

The hardest rockin' group around,
come catch us, playing live —
but get your ticket quick because
we tour on every tide!

Matt Goodfellow

The Friendly Octopus

Eight arms for me, eight arms for me,
I'm a friendly octopus, under the sea.

I've got

One arm to blow my nose,
One arm to wave with,
One arm to brush my teeth,
One arm to shave with,
One arm to comb my hair,
One arm to shake with,
One arm to blow a kiss,
And one to eat a cake with.

Eight arms for me, eight arms for me,
I'm a friendly octopus, under the sea.

Mike Jubb

Crab

Crab with a small brain
    Why do you
Go backward
    To go forward?
Is it my own world
    Is it your own world
That is upside down?
    Lucky you are not a car
Otherwise
    Oh dear, oh dear
You would have so many accidents!

Irene Assiba D'Almeida

28

Man on the Beach

Where is he going?
Where has he been?
Where does he come from?
What has he seen?
Why is he limping?
Is he in pain?
Why is he walking
alone in the rain?
Does he feel jolly?
Does he feel sad?
Does he have children?
Is he a dad?
Are his hands freezing?
Is his coat warm?
Why is he walking
alone in the storm?

Joshua Seigal

Further information

Websites

For web resources related to the subject of this book, go to:
www.windmillbooks.com/weblinks and select this book's title.

About the Poets:

Debra Bertulis' life-long passion is the written and spoken word, and she is the author of many published poems for children. She is regularly invited to schools where her workshops inspire pupils to compose and perform their own poetry. Debra lives in Herefordshire, England, where she enjoys walking the nearby Welsh hills and seeking out second-hand book shops!

Clare Bevan used to be a teacher until she decided to become a writer instead. So far, she has written stories, plays, song lyrics, picture books, and a huge heap of poetry. Her poems have appeared in over one hundred anthologies, and she loves performing them in schools. Her hobbies are reading and acting, and she once dressed up as a farmyard chicken.

James Carter is the liveliest children's poet and guitarist in town. He's traveled nearly everywhere from Loch Ness to Southern Spain with his guitar, Keith, to give performances and workshops in schools, libraries, and festivals.

Jane Clarke is the author of over 80 children's books including the award-winning picture books *Stuck in the Mud*, illustrated by Gary Parsons, and *Gilbert the Great*, illustrated by Charles Fuge. She's delighted to have a poem in this anthology.

Jan Dean likes ice cream and earrings. Her penguin earrings are special favorites. (Also the giraffes.) She likes singing, drawing and making bread. She visits schools to perform her poems and write new poems with classes. She likes it best when the poems explode all over the whiteboards and dribble down the walls…

Graham Denton is a writer and anthologist of poetry for children, whose poems are featured in numerous publications both in the UK and other countries. As an anthologist, his compilations include *Orange Silver Sausage: A Collection of Poems Without Rhymes*, *My Cat is in Love with The Goldfish*, and *When Granny Won Olympic Gold*. Most recently, Graham celebrated the release of the first full collection of his own funny verses, *My Rhino Plays The Xylophone*. He has also twice been short-listed for the UK's CLPE Poetry Award.

John Foster is a children's poet, anthologist, and poetry performer, well-known for his performance as a dancing dinosaur. He has written over 1,500 poems and *The Poetry Chest* containing over 250 of his own poems is published by Oxford University Press. He is a former teacher and the author of many books for classroom use.

Matt Goodfellow is a poet and primary school teacher from Manchester, England. His poems have been published in magazines and anthologies worldwide. Matt's high-energy performances and workshops have delighted, excited, and enthused thousands of children in schools, libraries, and bookshops across the UK.

Mike Jubb's poems are widely anthologized and he has a picture book, *Splosh*.

Tony Mitton has been published as a poet for children since the early '90s. He has also written many successful verse picture books and works blending poetry with narrative. He has won several awards. He lives in Cambridge, England, where he continues to read and write.

Brian Moses lives in Burwash, England where the famous writer Rudyard Kipling once lived. He travels the country performing his poetry and percussion show in schools, libraries and theaters. He has published more than 200 books including the series of picture books *Dinosaurs Have Feelings Too*. His favorite animal is his fox red labrador, Honey.

Joshua Seigal is a poet, performer, and educator who works with children of all ages and abilities. He has performed his poems at schools, libraries, and festivals around the country, as well as leading workshops designed to inspire confidence and creativity.

Ian Souter is retired from teaching and loves to exercise, play music, explore England, and travel. He lives in the wilds of Surrey, England, but also loves to visit, in particular, France and Australia. On his travels he also keeps an eye (and an ear) open for words and ideas. Sometimes he finds them hanging from trees or people's mouths or even sparkling in the sunshine.

Kate Williams When Kate's children were young, she made up poems to read them at bedtime. It was their clever idea that she send them off to a publisher, and she's been contributing to children's anthologies ever since! Kate finds writing a poem is like making a collage, but less sticky — except that she's stuck in the craze! She provides workshops for schools, too.

Index of first lines